A PART
OF THE DREAM

Text copyright 1992 by The Child's World, Inc.
All rights reserved. No part of this book may be
reproduced or utilized in any form or by any means
without written permission from the Publisher.
Printed in the United States of America.

Designed by Bill Foster of Albarella & Associates, Inc.

Distributed to schools and libraries
in the United States by
ENCYCLOPAEDIA BRITANNICA EDUCATIONAL CORP
310 South Michigan Ave.
Chicago, Illinois 60604

Library of Congress Cataloging-in-Publication Data
Bunting, Eve, 1928-
A part of the dream/Eve Bunting.
p. cm.
Summary: After her parents' divorce, Lisa and her
mother spend a week of vacation in Mexico.
ISBN 0-89565-771-6
[1. Mothers and daughters – Fiction. 2. Divorce –
Fiction. 3. Mexico – Fiction.] I. Title.
[PZ7.B91527Par 1991]
[Fic]—dc20
                                          91-15945
                                             CIP
                                             AC

Young Romance

A PART OF THE DREAM

Eve Bunting

Illustrated by

Lucyna A.M. Green

T H E   C H I L D ' S   W O R L D

*L*isa followed her mother off the bus and into the coolness of the hotel. The foyer swarmed with people in skimpy shorts, swimsuits, sundresses. There was a blur of color, the smell of suntan oil, a jumble of voices. Everyone seemed to be speaking English, which was a little disappointing. After all, this was Mexico, a foreign country. But then, the hotel guests would be mostly tourists, like themselves.

"Senora, Senorita." The hotel porter in his white shirt and pants piled their bags by a sleek desk, so highly polished that the dish of gardenias on it was reflected in the wood surface.

"Thank you," Lisa's mom said. "Gracias." She gave him the pesos she'd been holding since the second they'd left the airport. Usually Daddy took care of things like that, but Daddy wasn't around any more.

"That can't be. We reserved one of the ocean view rooms," her mom was saying now.

The Mexican lady behind the desk wore a red hibiscus tucked behind one ear and a snooty expression. "Senora!"

she spread out her hands with their long, red-tipped nails. "These things do happen sometimes. I apologize. But for you and your daughter I have a beautiful room. A little further back, perhaps, but quieter."

Lisa's mother turned to Lisa and said, "Can you believe it?"

This would never have happened if Daddy had been with them, Lisa thought quickly and her mother's mind must have been running on the same lines. Lisa saw her mouth tighten.

"We don't want a quieter room," she said. "We reserved a room on the beach and that is what we intend to get." There was something in the raised tone of her voice that made the lobby people stop chattering and turn to stare. Lisa saw the look on her mother's face and she thought, oh, oh! She put a hand on her arm. "It's OK, Mom. Maybe it would be better further back. We…"

"I want to see the manager," her mom said.

"Senora," the desk lady sighed. Her cold dark eyes held as much warmth as a lizard's.

Busboys in pleated shirts of pink and blue and yellow watched them warily.

The desk lady's finger hovered over a bell artfully recessed in the desk's dark wood, but before she could push it one of the busboys stepped forward.

"Momento," he said, and flashed a smile in Lisa's direction. He had hair so black that it looked blue and soft, warm skin against the pink of his shirt. He began talking to the desk lady, talking very fast with a great deal of handwaving and smiling. Lisa knew she was staring, but she couldn't help it. She'd never in her life seen anyone so handsome.

Her friends had teased her about her Mexican vacation. "Wow! Those Mexican guys have to be the best-looking anywhere," they'd said.

Lisa had shrugged. But it looked as if her friends were right.

The busboy was holding out his hand and the desk lady passed over a key. She snapped some words at him and he smiled as she swiveled her chair so her back was to them.

The lobby people went back to minding their own business.

"Senora! Senorita!" He held up the key. "A misunderstanding only. I have now a room for you, a suite, to be exact, with a terrace to the beach as you desired."

Lisa saw the stiffness drain from her mom and felt, rather than heard her sigh of relief. Mom really hated having to stand up to people.

"Oh, thank you," Mom said to the busboy. "We have been looking forward to being on the beach. It wouldn't have been the same."

"I agree. It would not have been the same." He dazzled his smile between them and his dark eyes moved from one of them to the other. There was something in those eyes, some kind of knowledge that made Lisa suddenly embarrassed. What did he know about them? About people like them?

He spoke to the pink and blue and yellow group who were all grinning and staring openly. One boy, younger than the others, came forward and loaded their bags onto a wheeled trolly.

"I am Carlos," he said. "It is room one hundred and thirty that I have for you. Please follow me."

He wheeled the trolly and Lisa and her mom walked behind him.

There was so much to see. The pool lay on their right across a strip of incredibly green grass. Music drifted from a striped cabana at one end, lazy guitar music with a Latin beat. Tan bodies splashed and swam in water so blue that it hurt Lisa to look at it, and she fumbled for her sunglasses that she'd pushed on top of her head and pulled them down over her eyes. On the left was a low hedge of tropical shrubs, scarlet and gold hibiscus, small fan-tailed palms, and beyond that lay the ocean and the golden sand of the beach.

Her mom smiled over one shoulder and murmured, "Wow!"

Wow indeed. So how come, when there was so much to admire was her core of attention focused on Carlos, walking ahead of them on the narrow path? She couldn't believe the color and texture of that hair, and the way he

walked, as if he owned the hotel, and everyone in it.

"We are here, Senora and Senorita." He flung open a door and stepped aside for them to enter. Going past him into the air-conditioned coolness Lisa was very conscious of him, of his darkness, blending against the rich polish of the carved door. He came quickly behind them to open the aqua blue drapes and suddenly the whole stretch of the beach, the vastness of the Pacific was there, just outside their window.

"Pretty, yes?" Carlos asked and he waved a hand, as though giving it to them as a gift, a welcome to Mexico.

He strode through the room that was all hot Mexican pinks and bright blues and opened another door. "The bathroom," he said. "The water is safe to drink. Our hotel has its own methods to make it agreeable to North American visitors." Again the smile. Lisa saw her mother respond to it, saw the tiredness of the plane and bus trip drop away from her.

"If there is anything you want or need, press the bell, Senora. Carlos will come."

"Thank you so much." Her mom was searching her purse again for another tip, her face pink with worry of it, wondering how much to give and how to give it graciously.

The note was probably too much. Carlos slipped it into his hand where it vanished as mysteriously as an egg in the hand of a magician.

"Gracias," he said. "And Senorita, if you will come with me I will show you the ice machine. The ice too is pure." He touched his stomach. "It will not upset what is inside."

"Oh, well." Lisa set her purse on the bed. "I'll find it later. No hurry." There was this strange reluctance to go with him.

"Believe me, Senorita, without me you will have trouble." His hand curved through the air. "It is to the left, then to the right, the left...or is it right again?"

"Better go, Lisa." Her mom kicked off her shoes and flopped on one of the beds.

Lisa looked up quickly and into his dark eyes. Something there. Something waiting.

"How come you speak such good English, Carlos?" her mom asked. "Have you been to the States?"

"Never, Senora. I have been in the hotel now for three summers. The Americans who come down, they teach me. They teach me a lot." Again the smile.

I'll bet, Lisa thought. I bet the American senoritas really enjoy teaching you English.

"We go," Carlos said.

The heat outside seemed stronger now after the chill of the room. Lisa felt perspiration on her upper lip and wiped it away with a fingertip.

"This way," Carlos said.

She followed him past the closed doors of other suites, past flowerbeds with great, waxy blossoms, perfect enough to be artificial.

Carlos stopped. "Look!" He caught her wrist.

An iguana pulsed in the shade of an oleander.

"Iguana," Carlos said. "The North Americans like them." His fingers stayed on her arm, strangely cool and dry against the heat of her skin.

"Gross!" Lisa said, and Carlos laughed and repeated the word. "Gross! That means ugly?"

"Ugly," Lisa said. She stepped back and his hand dropped from her arm.

"Here is the machine," Carlos said. He opened the lid, scooped out a plastic bowl of ice and offered it to her.

"Gracias," Lisa said. She wished

he'd let go of the bowl. There they stood, holding it between them.

"Do you like to dance?" Carlos asked.

For a second she thought she'd imagined words he'd never said. But when she made herself look at him she knew there'd been no mistake.

"Every night, on the beach, the mariachis play. It is for the guests only, you understand, Senorita?"

He let go of the bowl and she clutched it to her for protection. Ice water soaked into the front of her shirt, making her shiver.

"But there is a place, further along, where the music can still be heard. It is the place where the boats are pulled high. The sand there is always smooth and hard at night. Have you ever danced barefoot on a moonlit beach, Senorita? I guarantee it is something you will not forget."

Someone was coming, squeaking along in hurraches. It was a large man with the pinkest stomach Lisa had ever seen. He was carrying an empty bowl, the twin of hers.

"Howdy," he said. "Hot enough for you?"

"Hi," Lisa turned and walked quickly away.

"Right, then left, then right again, Senorita," Carlos called after her.

She knew that. She could have found the ice machine without his help too. And he'd known that right from the beginning.

*H*er mom was stretched out on the bed. "Isn't this fantastic?" She waved a hand at the beach outside their window. "And to think we might have been stuck in the back!" She glowed with satisfaction and Lisa knew her mom had already decided she'd done it all herself. That she was beginning to do OK without Dad.

"Well?" Her mom stretched her arms

high above her head. "What shall we do first? Unpack? Go to the beach?"

"The beach." Lisa set the ice down to melt away and rummaged in her case for her bikini.

Her mom had a bikini too, the very first one she'd ever owned. It went along with the other new things. The new colored hair; the dresses bought in Robinson's Teenwear department for the trip. It was easier for Lisa to understand the changes than to accept them. When you'd been divorced after eighteen years of marriage and then watched your husband remarry a lady of twenty-six, well it had to do something to your ego. Her mom had moped at first, and then she started going to some club where other divorced ladies counselled her. There was a thing they stressed called assertiveness training which, as far as Lisa could see, consisted of making yourself do what you didn't really want to do and wouldn't, if you were thinking straight. So here they were, Lisa and her new thinking Mom. But she had to admit this was a lot better than the moping stuff. And at least her mom's bikini was a size eight and not an eighteen.

They got their lotion and sunhats and beach walkers and helped themselves to two of the big, fluffy towels that hung on the bathroom rails.

It was neat to be able to slide open the door and step onto a private terrace and from there on to an infinite

stretch of golden sand.

"But there aren't any umbrellas free," Lisa's mom said. "You probably have to stake one out early in the day."

Lisa stared around. It was true. The thatched sunshades all had groups of people stretched out under their shadows. Under the one closest to them an old man sat reading.

"Do you think it would be OK to ask him to share?" Lisa's mom murmured.

"I don't think so," Lisa answered quickly.

She saw her mom's natural unassertiveness struggling with her training and she saw the training win. That training had been powerhouse stuff.

"Excuse me," her mom said.

The gray head lifted.

"My daughter and I wondered if we might share your umbrella. We've just arrived and I'm afraid we'll burn if we sit in the direct sun."

The man looked so astonished that Lisa knew at once this wasn't done. But he immediately put down his book and said, "Certainly. There's no sense at all in two people using shade that's quite adequate for four." He moved his chair a few feet.

"Thank you so much," Lisa's mom said and Lisa thought, two? What two?

As if in answer to her question a boy about a year older than she came running up from the ocean. He was tanned to the same deep dark brown as the man and he was wet and sleek as a seal. Tight little ringlets bobbed all over his head.

"This is my grandson, Tony," the man said. "I am William Westridge."

"Christine Patton, and my daughter, Lisa." She and Lisa spread their towels and sat on the sand. Tony unrolled a straw mat and sat next to Lisa.

"Did you just arrive?" he asked.

"Yes." Lisa watched him shake water from his hair. Little drops dimpled the sand around them. "Have you been here long?"

"Actually, we don't stay in the hotel," he said. "But Grandfather writes their advertising and brochures. So we're welcome to use all their facilities." He nodded at a small house perched on a clump of sand and coarse grass further down the beach. "That's Grandfather's house. I'm staying with him for the summer."

His grandfather smiled down at Lisa. "I call it my three hundred dollar house with the three hundred thousand dollar view."

"You mean, you live here all the time?" her mother asked.

Mr. Westridge nodded. "Since I retired."

Lisa let some of the white, powdery sand trickle through her fingers. Imagine living here all the time! Someone in a pink, pleated shirt and black pants moved quietly on the path between the beach and the hotel office and her heart gave an urgent lurch. Was it Carlos? No, no. That guy was too tall.

He didn't have the grace, the knowing way of walking. How could anyone have a knowing walk? Don't be dumb, Lisa. But he had. He knew girls were watching him. He knew what they were thinking. He knew how they felt about him.

Her mother was talking to Mr. Westridge.

Lisa got up on one elbow and looked along the beach. There was a raised bandstand, empty now. A shining wooden deck had been built around it. Lisa moved her head cautiously. "But there is a place, further along, where the music can still be heard. It is the place where the boats are pulled high." There they were. Two catamarans, three or four canoes. They lay almost in front of Mr. Westridge's house. Not that she had the slightest intention of going there anyway. What did he think she was? "Have you ever danced, barefoot, on a moonlit beach, Senorita?" She shivered.

Tony touched her arm with a sandy finger. "Goosebumps. You can't be cold."

Lisa laughed. "No. Somebody walking on my grave, that's all."

Mr. Westridge ordered them fruit drinks that came in a hollowed out pineapple and Lisa went swimming three times with Tony in water that was warmer than tepid.

The shadows from the thatched shelters stretched long across the sand before she and her mom gathered up their towels to leave.

"There's dancing every night," Tony told them. He pointed down toward the dance deck. "Think you'll go?" he asked Lisa casually. "I usually walk up."

"I guess so," Lisa said.

"I guarantee it's something you'll never forget," Carlos had said, but he was talking about up there, where the boats were, dancing, just the two of them.

"Goosebumps again," Tony said in amazement. "Your grave's getting some going over today!" He watched as they walked across the sand to their room. "Don't forget the dancing," he called after them. "You'll like it. It's real romantic."

"What isn't romantic here?" Lisa's mom asked later, when they were having dinner.

"I can't think of a thing," Lisa said.

*T*hey ate in the hotel dining room, the roof rolled back to show the moon and the sky full of stars. Candles floated in crystal bowls on the tables and there was the glow of phosphorous somewhere out in the deep darkness, where sea met sand.

They had Mexican food. Thin strips of pork served in a sauce of hot peppers and tomatoes. Lisa didn't see

Tony or his grandfather and she figured the welcome privileges didn't include meals in the dining room. She didn't see Carlos either, and she found herself wondering if he lived close by, or in the hotel itself. Did he only work days? How did he look, out of the uniform of pink shirt and black pants? She pictured him in jeans, a white turtleneck, and found she didn't feel like finishing the food on her plate.

After dinner they walked across to where the mariachi music melted into the softness of the tropical night and where dancing figures drifted, light as moths under the glow of the lanterns.

Someone asked her to dance. And a little later Tony came and asked her too, and sat at the table with them. He was nice, really nice, Lisa thought. But he was ordinary too. He was just like the guys at home. And that didn't seem too exciting anymore. Her eyes kept flicking to the dark beach and the ghostly white outlines of the catamarans, their tall masts slicing the velvet blackness of the sky.

Her mother was glowing. A man called Mark Cassidy had danced with her and now he had joined them at their table. Once Lisa and Tony passed them on the dance floor and she saw that they were moving together slowly and cheek to cheek. I don't like him, Lisa thought immediately. But maybe it's just that I resent anyone taking Dad's place, even for one dance. And that isn't fair to Mom.

38

Then, when Lisa and Tony came back to their table after a samba, she found her mother had disappeared.

Mark Cassidy smiled and blew cigarette smoke. "She had to run to the powder room," he said. "She's not feeling too good."

"What's the matter?" Lisa asked quickly.

"Montezuma's revenge, I'd say," Mark Cassidy said.

"Oh, oh," Tony groaned.

Lisa stared at him. "What is it? Montezuma's revenge?"

"Something tourists get often down here," Tony said. "It's the water. She'll be OK."

"But the water in the hotel is OK. He said so." Standing there, smiling that knowing smile, his black head gleaming.

Tony shrugged. "Well, it could be what she ate tonight. Anything."

Lisa went to the powder room to find her. And she was sick all right.

"I don't know if I'll be able to make it back to the room," she groaned. "Are you feeling OK, Lisa?"

"Great," Lisa said.

They refused Tony and Mark Cassidy's offer of help, and went back alone to their room.

Lisa helped her mom into bed.

"What a rotten way to end the evening," her mom said. "But you don't have to stay with me. You go out and have fun."

"No," Lisa said. "I'm pretty tired

myself."

But she went for a minute to stand on the terrace and think. The shadows of the catamarans seemed to beckon to her. The palms whispered, the sea murmured against the sand. The sweet sound of the music drifted on the soft air. "You'll never forget it," he'd said.

Lisa went inside and drew the drapes across to close out the magic of the night.

*H*er mom was still asleep when she wakened in the morning. Seven o'clock, and the sun already burning through the thickness of the drapes she'd closed with such finality last night.

She put on her bikini, took a towel and soundlessly opened the door.

There was no one in the pool area except a boy of about ten, dressed in a white shirt and pants who was placing gleaming ashtrays in the exact center of all the tables.

Lisa dived in and began lapping the pool, feeling the good silken pull of the water against her muscles. She came up at the end of the twelfth lap, slicking back her hair, and saw a blur of yellow standing by the steps.

She blinked. Carlos! A loose pleated shirt today that was the color of yellow daisies and pants, white as snow. He held out her towel.

Lisa climbed up the steps. He'll have to button up that shirt more before the other hotel guests see him, she thought vaguely and knew she was staring at the chain that hung around his neck. She'd never seen a chain with that much stuff hanging from it. It was amazing that he didn't jingle when he walked. There seemed to be rings and charms and identity discs. What on earth…?

"Good morning!" He handed her the towel and smiled that heart stopping smile. "Last night. It was such a beautiful night. I waited and I waited, but the little Lisa did not come."

Lisa wrapped the towel around her. "My mom was sick," she said. "I have to go now and see how she is."

"Ah, the poor mother. It is the Turistas? Today, she will be better, you will see. And tonight I will be there again, by the boats, hoping that the little Lisa will come and share the time with me."

Lisa wriggled her feet into her sandals. She'd never known her name could sound that soft and pretty. And how did he know it anyway?

"You will come?"

If only a nice fat, pink man would come along again and save her.

"I don't know," Lisa said, and she ran past him and back to her room.

Her mom was up and feeling better. They spent the morning on the beach and in the afternoon they went on a city tour, walking through the exotic food market, driving to the cliffs to watch the divers plunge into the swell of the waves, way, way down below. But Lisa's mind kept wandering, wandering and she knew she resented the time away from the magic of the Mazatlan Hotel.

That night they danced again in the glow of the lanterns. Tony found Lisa and they sat on the low sea wall and then walked together on the beach where little sea crabs crawled on their nightly pilgrimage from the sea. Tony kissed her. It was nice. But she was careful that they didn't stray close to the place where the boats were pulled high, and she was careful too to keep the image of Carlos pushed in the back of her mind…the image of the way it would be, dancing with him there on the edge of the ocean.

The next day they took the jungle tour, gliding along the dark river where blue herons flew, chilling to the sounds of the jungle that crowded the river on either side. Mark Cassidy was with them, sitting between Lisa and her mother, holding her mom's hand. Lisa saw her mother's returning self-assurance that had nothing to do with her assertiveness training and everything to do with him. She fought her dislike for him the way she fought her own attractions for Carlos.

She saw Carlos often, but always at a distance. He'd be standing on the flower-bordered path when she and her mother left the dining room and he'd smile that smile that added excitement to the day. Once he was the one who carried their cold drinks to them as they sat by the pool.

"It's Carlos!" Lisa's mom said.

"I volunteer," Carlos said. Lisa wondered how the sun could seem instantly brighter, the morning sweeter.

The week was passing.

On the last day Mr. Westridge invited them for lunch. They sat outside, the four of them, eating tostados and tiny, succulent taquitos and drinking ice cold papaya juice.

"Fiesta tonight," Tony told them. "Friday evening at the Hotel Mazatlan is something special, you'll see."

"Every day and every evening at the Hotel Mazatlan is special," Lisa's mother said. "How could it possibly be better?"

"You'll see," Tony said again.

And that night, coming out of the room and walking the path to the dining room they did see.

A buffet supper was laid out under long, striped awnings. Whole lobsters gleamed pinkly on beds of ice. Giant coral shrimp curled heads to tails against delicate poached salmon. There were cartwheels of avocados, stuffed with crab. Gleaming fruits and berries were piled high in crystal bowls.

Tony detached himself from a group as soon as Lisa and her mom appeared.

"Didn't I tell you?" he asked.

"But where did all the people come from. I haven't seen a tenth of them before," Lisa's mom said.

"It's open season tonight. Not just hotel guests. Half of Maztlan is here."

Lisa looked around. What about the hotel staff? The ones who worked days and were off duty at night? There was a nervous fluttering somewhere inside her. She wanted him to be here. But she was nervous too. She'd been nervous about him all along. He wasn't here. One quick check told her that. There was something about him that made him visible to her instantly. And there was a tingling that came, a sort of radar that warned her of his closeness.

But the radar failed her after all.

She was dancing with a boy called Ford Taylor. He was telling her how he'd gone on a two-hour fishing trip and almost caught a marlin big as a whale. "You usually see those big marlin further out," he said. "I've been thinking about taking a full-day boat, really going after one. But, man, they charge a fortune for those whole day jobs and…" He stopped in mid-sentence.

"Excuse me," a voice said. A Mexican-American-English voice.

"Darn. Someone's cutting in," Ford muttered. "I'll be back."

Then Carlos had his arms around her and he was moving her through the crowd of dancers.

She couldn't breathe. She couldn't speak. She couldn't think.

She'd imagined the way he would look in outside clothes, and she'd pictured him in a white turtleneck, his blue-black hair thick against the roll of the collar. But it was too hot, of course. His shirt was creamy beige, the pull-on kind with buttons. She saw the gleam of the silver chain against his throat. His lips were close to her ear.

"I should not be here. But tomorrow, you will leave. Will you come, Lisa? Will you come to the beach?"

She was melting, crumbling.

He held her a little away. "You think I am…gross? That is the reason you have not come?"

The word broke the spell and made her laugh. "No," she said. "You certainly are not gross."

Ford hovered behind him. Any second now he would cut in.

"I will wait," Carlos said.

There was something in his face that she couldn't place. Understanding moved on the edge of her mind, then drifted away as Ford tapped Carlos' shoulder and took over again.

"You know, I think that guy works here," Ford said. "He probably isn't even supposed to be dancing." He stopped. "Well, like I was saying, I'm sorry now that I didn't take that all-day boat. I'll be kicking myself when I get home." He grinned. "What the heck. I'm hoping to come back next year. I'll have another chance."

Lisa's eyes searched the room, but Carlos was gone. Was he out there already, waiting by the boats that gleamed, white in the moonlight?

*I*t was past midnight now. It was morning, her last morning in Mazatlan. Tomorrow night, she and her mom would be home. Would she be like Ford Taylor who hadn't taken the all-day boat? Would she think about dancing barefoot on the night beach and would she be kicking herself for letting it all slip away?

She went outside as if she were

sleepwalking. Seafoam lay creamy on the beach, thick and glistening. Carlos was a shadow, moving toward her from the deeper shadows.

It was dream music they danced to. The palm trees whispered against the dark of the sky and the sea murmured its secrets to the pale gold of the sand.

When the music faded to silence she knew that he'd kiss her. He held her a little away.

"I thought you would not come," he said, and there was that something in his voice that she'd heard before.

He led her to one of the gleaming pontoons of the largest catamaran and they sat side by side, facing the ocean.

"Tomorrow you will go." His finger touched the small silver heart that

dangled from her charm bracelet. His voice was mournful. "You will leave me this, so that I will always remember?"

Lisa sat very still.

"I will wear it around my neck," he said. "I will keep it always."

She looked into his face and understood. It was as if someone had kicked her, low in her stomach. All those souvenirs, given to him by senoritas who had come to dance with him on the night beach! They were scalps on his belt. His own kind of blue ribbons to hang on his wall. And he'd been afraid she was going to get away. But in the end, of course, she'd come.

"To remember you," he said, and the edge of worry was back in his voice. She had a quick vision of him counting off the trophies to his friends. "This one from Kate. This one from Linda. And the heart…the heart was Lisa's."

She pulled away from the touch of his hand. "You…you creep!" She whispered, then she was running, running from the boats and from him. She found their terrace through her tears and flung herself face down on the bed.

The sound of the music was poison now and she jammed her pillow hard against her ears to get away from it. How could he? How could he use them all like that?

She heard her mother's voice out-side, and Mark Cassidy's too. Then there was a small silence and the door slid open.

"Goodnight Mark," her mother called. "See you in the morning."

Lisa heard her close the door. Then the light came on.

"Lisa! I didn't know you were here!"

Lisa sat up.

"You've been crying!" There was understanding in her mom's voice. "It is hard to think we're leaving tomorrow. But that's the way vacations are. They have to come to an end."

She came across and sat by Lisa and put an arm around her. "It's been great though, hasn't it? I feel…I don't know…so much better."

Lisa pushed her hair back, "Aren't you sorry to leave Mark?"

"Well, sure. We helped each other have a better vacation. I like him a lot." She lowered her voice. "But I'll tell you the truth. If we'd met each other at home we probably wouldn't have noticed one another. But…he made this week special for me. I think we made it special for each other. And maybe that's enough." She got up and began to undress. "Oh, by the way. Tony couldn't figure out where you disappeared to. He said he'll be up in the morning to say goodby."

Lisa took off her bracelet and set it on the tiled dresser. The little heart winked at her. But something her mom had said had eased the hurt already. She needed to think about it.

Later, she lay in bed, trying to

understand.

Carlos! She remembered the beauty of his face, his glow, the way he'd made each day shimmer with its own special excitement. He wasn't a creep! The girls who'd come to share his beach had been searching for a dream, as she had. Carlos had given them his magic. He'd made the week special for all of them. What more did they want from him?

She thought about Tony. If only Carlos hadn't been around...! But he had been, and she was glad. It would be foolish to regret a dream.

Quietly she got up, unlatched the silver heart from its chain, found an envelope and slipped the heart inside. On the outside she wrote, "Carlos."

She'd leave it at the desk in the morning. Carlos would understand.